The Very Clever Aliens

by Joan Stimson

Illustrated by Rob McClurkan

W
FRANKLIN WATTS
LONDON•SYDNEY

About this book

Rhymes to Read are designed for children who are ready to start reading alone. They can also be used by an adult to share with a child.

The books provide excellent support for developing phonological awareness, helping the child to recognise sounds and sound-symbol relationships. The poems are perfect to read aloud and the strong rhythms, rhymes and repetition will help build confidence and encourage reading and rereading for pleasure.

Reading tips for adults sharing the book with a child:
1. Make reading fun! Choose a time to read when you and the child are relaxed and have time to share the story.
2. Talk about the story before you start reading. Look at the cover and the blurb. What might the story be about? Why might the child like it?
3. Encourage the child to retell the story, using the pictures and rhymes to help. The puzzles at the back of the book provide a good starting point.
4. Give praise! Remember that small mistakes need not always be corrected.
5. For an extra activity, you could ask the child to make up some alternative rhymes for the story or their own brand new rhyme!

There's something
we must say.

We're very clever aliens
and we are on our way.

Zooming high,
zooming high,
our spaceship
is the best.

We fly it
very cleverly
and never
take a rest.

Getting close,
getting close.
We'll soon be
in your street.

We know just
what we want –
it's something
good to eat!

BAKERY

Open up! Open up!
And give us all
your cake.

We're very clever aliens,
who don't know
how to bake.

Look out, **OUCH!**
Look out, **OUCH!**

12

13

The Cooks are
fighting back.
Their rolling pins are
very hard
and give
a mighty ...

OK, Cooks, OK, Cooks.
We'll do just
what you say.

We'll learn to bake
our own cupcakes
and then be on our way.

Thank you, Cooks,
thank you, Cooks,
for all our yummy cake.

We're very clever aliens,
who now know
how to bake.

MARTIAN MUFFINS

Puzzle 1

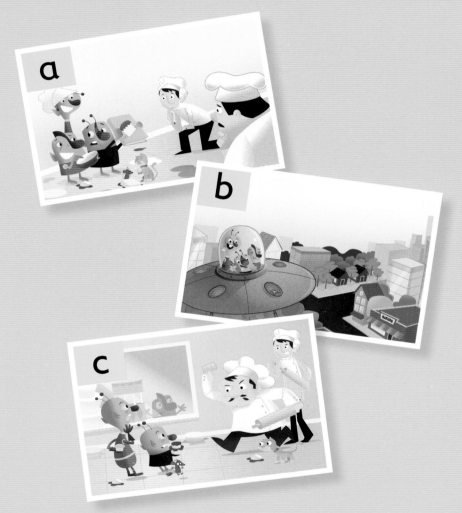

Put the pictures in the correct
order and retell the story.

Puzzle 2

cake

cook

bake

cat

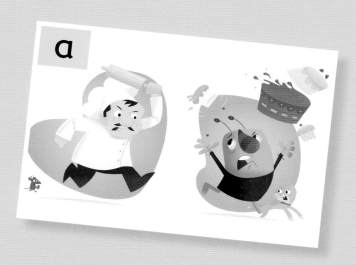

best

zoom

fly

rest

Find the rhyming words above.

Turn over for answers!

Answers

Puzzle 1

The correct order is: b, c, a.

Puzzle 2

The rhyming words are:

a. bake, cake

b. best, rest

First published in 2011 by
Franklin Watts
338 Euston Road
London
NW1 3BH

Franklin Watts Australia
Level 17/207 Kent Street
Sydney
NSW 2000

Text © Joan Stimson 2011
Illustration © Rob McClurkan 2011

The rights of Joan Stimson to be
identified as the author and Rob McClurkan
as the illustrator of this Work have been
asserted in accordance with the Copyright,
Designs and Patents Act, 1988.

A CIP catalogue record for this book is
available from the British Library.

ISBN 978 1 4451 0296 2 (hbk)
ISBN 978 1 4451 0303 7 (pbk)

Series Editor: Melanie Palmer
Series Advisor: Catherine Glavina
Series Designer: Peter Scoulding

Printed in China

Franklin Watts is a division of Hachette Children's Books,
an Hachette UK company. www.hachette.co.uk